What field trip would you like to go on?

I want to go apple-picking with Isadora Moon!
– Elinor

Dave Land, where everyone is called Dave.
– Oscar

To the science museum to play.
– Awel

To Legoland!
– Avery

I would like to go to a farm.
– Livia

Sink your fangs into an
Isadora Moon adventure!

Coming Soon!

ISADORA MOON

Goes on a Field Trip

Harriet Muncaster

A STEPPING STONE BOOK™
Random House 🏠 New York

For vampires, fairies, and humans everywhere!
And for my own little Honeyblossom,
Celestine Stardust.

Copyright © 2017 by Harriet Muncaster
Cover art copyright © 2017 by Harriet Muncaster

All rights reserved. Published in the United States by Random House
Children's Books, a division of Penguin Random House LLC, New York.
Originally published in paperback by Oxford University Press,
Oxford, in 2017.

Random House and the colophon are registered trademarks and
A Stepping Stone Book and the colophon are trademarks of
Penguin Random House LLC.

Visit us on the Web!
rhcbooks.com

Educators and librarians, for a variety of teaching tools,
visit us at RHTeachersLibrarians.com

Library of Congress Cataloging-in-Publication Data is available upon request.
ISBN 978-1-9848-5172-7 (pbk.)—ISBN 978-1-9848-5173-4 (ebook)

MANUFACTURED IN CHINA
10 9 8 7 6 5 4
First American Edition

This book has been officially leveled by using the
F&P Text Level Gradient™ Leveling System.

Random House Children's Books supports the
First Amendment and celebrates the right to read.

ISADORA MOON

Goes on a Field Trip

Chapter One

Isadora Moon, that's me! And this is Pink Rabbit. He comes everywhere with me. Even on field trips! I have only ever been on one field trip before—we went to the ballet—so I was very excited when our teacher, Miss Cherry, said that we would be going on another one!

"Oh, lovely," said Mom when I brought the permission slip home. "A historic castle museum! That will be interesting. Would you like Dad and me to volunteer again?"

"Um . . . ," I began. Mom and Dad had volunteered on my last field trip and it had been fine (mostly), but I am always a little unsure about them offering to help out. The thing is that my mom is a fairy and my dad is a vampire (which makes me a vampire-fairy, by the way). They are not like other parents, and sometimes it can be embarrassing.

"You can," I said. "If you really want to. Except Miss Cherry said they only need one volunteer this time. So only one of you can come."

"Oh," said Mom, looking slightly disappointed. "That's a shame. Your dad should go, then. You know how much he loves old castles!"

"I do!" agreed Dad, who was bouncing my baby sister, Honeyblossom, up and down. "I would love to go!" He whipped a pen out from underneath his cloak and briskly signed the letter.

Dear Parent,

Please sign to give your child permission to visit the historic castle museum on January 20. We will also need one parent volunteer to join us.

Sincerely,
Miss Cherry

Signed: Count Bartholomew Hart

"I hope I will get to wear one of those fashionable safety vests again," he said. "It was a very striking look."

"Yes," agreed Mom. "You did look handsome in it. They were nice and bright, weren't they? I think the word for that is 'fluorescent.'"

"Fluorescent!" said Dad. "I love that word!" He handed the letter back to me. "I can't wait for the trip!" he exclaimed. "Old castles are the best. Do you think it will be haunted? I hope so!"

"I don't know," I replied. "I'll have to ask Miss Cherry."

Chapter Two

"Haunted?!" said Miss Cherry in surprise when I asked her the question the next day at school. "Of course the castle won't be haunted! You shouldn't be worried about that!"

"I'm not worried," I said. "I just—"

"Haunted?" asked my friend Zoe. "Did you say the castle was haunted, Isadora?"

"No, I was just—"

"It's haunted!" cried Zoe loudly, putting her hand over her mouth in shock. "Oh my goodness!"

"Eek!" cried Samantha, wide-eyed. "I'm scared of ghosts!"

"Everyone's scared of ghosts!" said Bruno.

"The castle is haunted!" shouted Jasper.

Soon the whole class was in an uproar. Samantha's face had gone very white.

"Now, calm down, everyone," said Miss Cherry loudly. "The castle is NOT haunted."

"But what if it is?" squeaked Samantha.

"It's NOT," sighed Miss Cherry, rolling her eyes.

But no one in the class was listening. The idea that the castle was haunted had firmly planted itself into everyone's head.

"I bet the ghost wanders around the castle, wailing and moaning," said Zoe.

Sashi shivered. "I bet it has red, glowing eyes and very sharp teeth."

"I bet it eats children for breakfast," said Bruno.

"Oh, help!" gulped Samantha, trembling.

"Now, Dad," I said the night before the school trip. "I know you're a vampire, but you have to make sure you don't oversleep tomorrow. We need to be at school at nine o'clock to catch the bus."

"A bus!" said Dad. "How exciting! I have never been on one of those before."

He patted my arm. "And don't worry, Isadora, I will make sure I am ready. I am planning to set five extremely loud alarms. The first one will go off at five o'clock. That will give me about two and a half hours to do my hair. It's not much, I know, but it will have to do."

"Great!" I said happily. "Thanks, Dad."

"Oh my," said Mom. "Five alarms! I will have to magic up some special earplugs for myself tonight!"

"Don't worry, Mom," I said. "You can sleep in my room tonight. We can set up the camp bed! Maybe we can even roast marshmallows, like we did when we went camping!"

Mom laughed. "That's very sweet of you, Isadora," she said. "But I don't mind really. It's nice to be awake at the crack of dawn sometimes. Nature is very beautiful in the early morning."

"Oh, okay," I said, feeling a little bit

disappointed. "Could we still have some marshmallows, though? We could have them for dessert tonight!"

"Great idea!" said Mom, glancing out the window at the wet weather. "I do love being out in the fresh, sparkling rain!"

"Um . . . ," began Dad.

"I'll use magic to make us a shelter," said Mom. "That way the campfire won't go out."

Dad looked worried. He hates the rain because it messes up his perfectly groomed vampire hair.

"Do you think we could cook the marshmallows indoors?" he suggested. "Over the stove?"

"Oh, no!" said Mom, horrified. "We don't want to miss this glorious weather!"

Dad and I stared out the window at the darkening gray sky as Mom got things ready for the campfire. Rain was now pouring down in sheets.

"I hope it will clear up for the trip tomorrow," said Dad. "Otherwise we're going to get very wet."

"I'm sure it will," said Mom confidently. "It's probably just a little shower."

But we roasted our marshmallows under the magical shelter, and by the time we all went to bed, the rain was *still* hammering down on the roof of our house.

Chapter Three

When I woke up in the morning, it looked even grayer than it had the night before.

"Oh no," I said to Pink Rabbit as I hopped out of bed. "I think we're going to need raincoats today!"

Pink Rabbit shivered and looked worried. He hates getting wet, because he is made of stuffing. I opened my wardrobe door and pulled out his little plastic rain cape.

"You'll be fine if you wear this," I said, putting it on him. "You'll stay perfectly dry! And it looks very stylish."

Pink Rabbit looked cozy. He bounced up and down in front of the mirror, posing like a fashion model while I put on my own clothes. Then we both made our way downstairs to the kitchen.

Dad was already there, drinking his red juice.  His hair looked perfectly sleek and vampire-y, and he was wearing his best black waterproof cape. "I told you I would be ready." He yawned. He hurriedly put on his sunglasses to hide the dark rings under his eyes.

"Well done, Dad!" I said, sitting down at the table and reaching for a piece of toast.

"I'm not too sure about the weather, though," continued Dad. He glanced anxiously out the window. "It's pouring! I hate getting my hair messed up in the rain."

I looked at the black clouds outside and at the raindrops running in streaks down the window.

"We will have to take umbrellas," I said.

"Ah, yes!" said Dad, suddenly cheering up. "I can use my new, fancy black one with the pointed top!"

"And I can use my umbrella with the bat ears!" I said excitedly.

After breakfast we went into the hall and put on our rainboots. Dad grabbed his umbrella, and I put on my pink plastic rain cape with the hood.

"We're off!" Dad said, giving Mom a kiss on the cheek.

"Bye, Mom! Bye, Honeyblossom!" I said. We stepped out of the house.

"The rain can't touch me!" said Dad happily, twirling his enormous black umbrella above his head. "Don't we look fashionable!"

Pink Rabbit nodded in agreement as he splashed along beside me in his rubber boots.

21

Chapter Four

When we arrived at the school, we saw Miss Cherry standing outside on the sidewalk next to a big bus. She had a clipboard in one hand and an umbrella in the other.

"Ah, Mr. Moon!" she said as Dad and I came toward her. "You're here! Wonderful!" She put her clipboard under her arm and rummaged in her bag for a moment. "Here you are!" she said, holding out a fluorescent safety vest. "You need to put this on. It's required."

Dad took the vest gleefully. "Oh goody,"

he said. "I was looking forward to wearing this again. It's very stylish, don't you think?"

"Um . . . ," said Miss Cherry. "If you think so, Mr. Moon."

"I do!" said Dad. "Honestly, I'm just too stylish for words sometimes. I should be careful I don't get snapped up by a modeling agency."

Miss Cherry coughed awkwardly. "You can board the bus now" was all she said.

Dad put his umbrella down in a flurry of raindrops and stepped onto the bus. I followed him, and Pink Rabbit bounced in behind me.

"Isadora!" shouted Zoe from the back seat. "Come and sit next to me!"

I made my way to the back of the bus and sat down next to Zoe. She was bundled up in a raincoat with frog eyes on the hood.

"Are you nervous?" she asked as I made myself comfortable.

"Nervous?" I asked. "What do you mean?"

"About the ghost!" said Samantha, popping up from a seat in front of us and staring with wide, frightened eyes. "You know, the one in the castle!"

"Oh, that," I said. "I don't think—"

"It's going to be **TERRIFYING!**" said Bruno from a few rows down. "It's lucky I remembered my ghost-protector spray." He held up a little pink sparkly bottle, which looked suspiciously like perfume, and spritzed a cloud of something sickly sweet into the air.

Oliver wrinkled his nose. "That smells like perfume," he said. "It's the same bottle my mom uses."

"It's not perfume," said Bruno. "It's ghost-protector spray. Here, let me spray some on you."

"NO! NO!" shouted Oliver. "It smells like roses!"

"I'll use some," said Zoe. "Spray some on me!"

Bruno leaned across the seat and spritzed his ghost-protector spray all over Zoe. And then Sashi. And then Samantha.

"Do you want some, Isadora?" he asked.

"Yes, please," I said. I didn't really believe in Bruno's ghost-protector spray, but I did want to smell like roses too.

Just then Miss Cherry stepped up into the bus, with the remaining students following close behind her.

"At last!" she said. "We are all here! Bruno, sit down, please. Put your seat belts on, everyone. Let's go!"

There was a lot of clicking as we all did as Miss Cherry said, and then the bus rumbled to life. Miss Cherry sat down next to Dad and sniffed the air.

"It smells like roses in here," she said,

turning to the driver. "What a lovely air freshener!"

The bus pulled away from the school, and I looked out the window at the shiny road below. It seemed very far away.

"I didn't know buses could be so big!" I said to Zoe.

But Zoe wasn't listening. She was busy talking to Samantha and Sashi about the ghost.

"We all need to stick together," Sashi was saying. "That way, if it attacks, we will be safer."

"Good idea," said Zoe.

Samantha nodded, her face as white as a sheet. "Oh dear, oh dear," she squeaked.

Chapter Five

By the time we arrived at the castle museum, my friends had worked themselves up so much about the ghost that none of them wanted to leave the bus.

"Come on, kids!" said Miss Cherry impatiently. "What's wrong with you all? There is NO ghost in the museum."

Then Dad's head popped up from behind his seat.

"Oh, that's a shame," he said. "I love a good haunted castle."

Eventually, after much persuading from Miss Cherry, everyone got off the bus, even Samantha. We all stood on the side of the road as the bus pulled away. Everyone stared up at the castle museum in front of us. Huge black towers rose into the gray sky, and thunder and lightning cracked overhead.

"It definitely looks haunted," said Bruno.

"You're right!" said Dad happily. "Maybe it is, after all!"

Miss Cherry frowned. "That is not

a very helpful comment, Mr. Moon," she whispered. "The castle is most definitely NOT haunted! Now follow me, everyone."

We all followed Miss Cherry to the heavy black castle doors. Just beyond the doors was a ticket booth with a man sitting inside it.

"Ah," he said when he saw us. "You must be the students we are expecting today."

"Yes, we are," said Miss Cherry. "We have come for an educational visit."

"Excellent," said the man. He handed Miss Cherry a leaflet with a map of the castle on it and gestured toward the entrance to the first room.

"Have fun!" he said.

"I don't want to go in," whispered Sashi as Miss Cherry hurried us into the first room.

"Me neither." Samantha shivered. "This castle feels spooky."

"It's only spooky because of the weather," said Miss Cherry as a crash of thunder boomed overhead and a flash of lightning lit up the room. The whole class screamed except for me and Dad and Miss Cherry. I don't mind thunder and lightning. I am half-vampire, after all.

"Quiet, everyone," said Miss Cherry, beginning to sound a bit frazzled. "The thunder and lightning won't hurt you. Now, look at this beautiful historic room!"

We looked. It was a beautiful room. The ceiling was midnight black with silver stars painted on it, and there were two jeweled thrones sitting in the middle of the floor. Miss Cherry consulted the map.

"This is the throne room," she told us. "And look over there at all those crowns!"

Miss Cherry led us toward a big glass case that was full of glittering crowns. There were tall ones and short ones and spiky ones, and all of them were covered in diamonds.

"Wow," said Dad admiringly.

"I want to try one on!" said Zoe.

"You can't try these on," said Miss Cherry. "They're much too delicate. But look, there's a dress-up box over there. You can try on the costumes a king and queen would have worn in the olden days."

"I want to be a queen!" cried Zoe as she bolted toward the dress-up box. She rummaged inside it. "Ooh, look at this beautiful crown!"

"I'll be a king," said Oliver, taking out a long red cape with black-and-white-spotted fur trim.

"I want to be something," said Bruno. "But there are only two costumes in the box."

"There should be costumes to try on in every room," explained Miss Cherry. "You will all get a chance to dress up. By the time we've been through every room, you should each be wearing medieval outfits. The challenge is to find every costume in the castle!"

Chapter Six

"Ooh," said Dad. "How exciting!"

"Not for you, I'm afraid," said Miss Cherry. "The costumes are all in children's sizes."

"Oh," said Dad, sounding disappointed. "Oh well. I've got my safety vest at least!"

We all started to move toward the next room. My friends seemed to have forgotten about the ghost for the time being. They were busy chatting about the different costumes we might find in the castle's rooms.

Zoe walked proudly next to me in her jeweled royal dress and glittering crown. "I wish I could wear this every day!" she said.

Miss Cherry led us out of the throne room and into a long, gloomy hallway where there were flickering candles stuck all along the walls.

"This is my kind of place," said Dad as thunder cracked overhead again.

"Eek! What's that?" squealed Samantha after lightning lit up the whole hallway for a second, revealing a tall metal figure standing against the wall.

"That's a suit of armor," said Miss Cherry. "Knights used to wear armor to go into battle."

"Cool!" said Bruno. "Maybe there's a knight outfit somewhere." He raced toward the dress-up box at the end of the hallway and flung the lid open.

"TWO suits of armor!" he shouted, holding up two clinking silver costumes. "Who wants to be a knight with me?"

"Me!" shouted Jasper.

"Me!" shouted Sashi.

"You can't be a knight—you're a girl, Sashi," said Bruno.

"I CAN!" said Sashi, snatching the suit before Jasper could get to it. She hurriedly put it on. "Girls can be knights too!"

"Of course they can," said Dad. "Bruno and Sashi do look cool, don't they? All that shiny, gleaming metal. Maybe I should get a metal vampire cape!"

At the end of the hallway there was a flight of steps.

"This leads down into the dungeon," explained Miss Cherry, looking at her map. "It's where they used to keep the prisoners."

"Oh no!" wailed Samantha, biting her fingers nervously. "That's exactly the kind of place a ghost would be hiding."

"Wonderful," exclaimed Dad. "I'll go first!" He started to make his way down the steps, and Pink Rabbit, Miss Cherry, and I followed him. The rest of the class trailed behind reluctantly.

"Don't forget," I heard Bruno say, "you'll be safe if you've got your ghost-protector spray on."

The dungeon was dark and cold, with no windows. Candles flickered on the walls all around us, making shapes loom up in the dim light. Even I gave a little shiver and held on tightly to Pink Rabbit's paw.

"Very atmospheric," said Dad, looking around. "This is the kind of effect I am always trying to create in my bathroom. I love candlelit baths."

"Hmm," said Miss Cherry. "It's maybe a little too atmospheric. Should we go back upstairs now? There are lots of other things to see. There's a tall tower somewhere, with one hundred twirly steps leading up to it."

"Ooh!" said Jasper. "I'd like to go up there!"

"Me too!" said Bruno.

The class began to make its way back upstairs, but Dad lingered behind.

"What's in there?" he asked, pointing at a small door in the wall. "Should we open it?"

"Um . . . ," I began. The last of my classmates disappeared up the dungeon steps.

"Come on," said Dad. "We can always catch up to the others. Let's take a quick look!"

Chapter Seven

Dad hurried across the room and pulled open the door. A cloud of dust billowed into the air, and spiders scuttled across the floor. Pink Rabbit jumped in alarm. He hates spiders.

"I don't think there's anything in there, Dad," I said as we peered into the dark space behind the door. "I think it's just a cupboard."

"Hmmm," said Dad, peering closer and brushing away the spiderwebs. "But what's that?" He pointed up into one corner where there was something shadowy and silvery all curled up.

"OH . . . ," I said, staring at it in wonder. "Is it? Is it . . . ?"

"A ghost!" said Dad. "Yes! I think it is!"

Little shivers went all the way up and down my spine. I had never seen a real ghost before, even though Dad talks about them all the time.

Suddenly, I felt a little afraid.

"Shut the door again, Dad," I said. "I don't think we should disturb it."

"Nonsense!" said Dad as the ghost began to uncurl itself in the corner of the cupboard. "Look—it's friendly!"

But I didn't think the ghost looked very friendly. It raised its shimmery, glimmery arms up into the air and opened its mouth into a wide O shape.

"OOOooohhh!" it moaned.

I put my hands over my eyes.

"It's just pretending," laughed Dad. "I can do that too! OOOoooohh!"

I peeked out from behind my fingers and saw that the ghost was looking very surprised.

"OOOOOoooooooOOOOOOHHHHH!" he wailed again, but this time much more loudly.

"OOOOOoooooooOOOOOOHHHHH!" copied Dad.

The ghost looked upset. He crossed his silvery arms in front of his chest and frowned.

"You are supposed to run away when I do

that," the ghost said. "That's what usually happens."

"Oh, really?" asked Dad. "But I thought we could have a nice chat!"

"A chat?" said the ghost. "I haven't had one of those in years! Two hundred, to be exact."

Dad looked horrified. "Two hundred years!" he exclaimed. "You mean to say you haven't spoken to anyone in **TWO HUNDRED YEARS?!**"

The ghost hung his head sadly.

"You must have been very lonely," continued Dad.

"I have been lonely," said the ghost, giving a little sniff. "I used to try to talk to people, but they always ran away screaming, so in the end I gave up. Now I just try to scare them on purpose instead. It's much easier because that's what people expect from a ghost."

"Mmm." Dad nodded.

"Mostly, though," continued the ghost, "I hide in the cupboard. I don't really like scaring people, and sometimes they throw things at me."

"Oh dear . . . ," soothed Dad. "That can't be fun."

"It's not," said the ghost. "I just wish people could see me for who I am and not *what* I am."

"Understandable," said Dad, stroking his chin thoughtfully. "Well, I'm sure it can't be too hard to get people to see that you're friendly. Why don't you come with us? We're on a field trip, and we could introduce you to the rest of the class. I'm sure none of them would be scared of you once we explain who you are. What's your name?"

"Oscar," said the ghost, holding out his cold, silvery hand for Dad and me to shake. I took his hand, but it didn't feel solid at all. It was like shaking hands with a cloud!

"Okay, Oscar," said Dad. "You just come with us. "We'll introduce you to everyone!"

Oscar seemed unsure, but he floated out of the cupboard and followed Dad and me across the dungeon floor. As we neared the stone steps, I noticed a dress-up box standing against the wall in the corner.

"Wait!" I said, running over to it. "Let's see what costumes are in this room!"

I opened the box and pulled out a black-and-white-striped jumpsuit.

"A prisoner costume!" I said.

"Oh, that is nice," said Dad. "I am a fan of black-and-white stripes. You should put it on, Isadora. It would match Pink Rabbit's raincoat!"

I rushed to pull the jumpsuit on over my clothes. Attached to one of the ankles was a papier-mâché ball and chain, which dragged along the ground when I walked.

Oscar shivered. "I remember the days when there were real prisoners down here," he said.

The three of us made our way back up the dungeon steps and into the hallway above. As we walked, I started to feel uneasy.

"Dad," I said, tugging on his sleeve, "I think the class might be scared of Oscar if we just turn up with him like this. Maybe we should introduce him to the others in a different way?"

Oscar looked sad when I said this, but I didn't want him to feel offended when all my friends started screaming.

"Don't be silly," said Dad. "Who could be scared of Oscar? He's such a friendly

ghost. No, we'll just introduce him to the class and explain that he's our friend."

"But—" I said.

"It will be fine, Isadora," Dad insisted. "Don't worry."

Oscar seemed reassured. He even started to smile! But his smile didn't last for long. We rounded the corner and I saw Miss Cherry and my classmates all standing in a group. Miss Cherry was ticking off names on a clipboard and looking confused.

"I am sure we are missing two people and a pink rabbit . . . ," she was saying.

Then she looked up and saw us. All my friends looked up and saw us.

And then they **SCREAMED**.

Every single one of them.

Even Miss Cherry.

Chapter Eight

"AAAARRRGGGGHHHHHH!!!!"
she shouted, dropping her clipboard on the floor and turning as white as a ghost herself.

"EEEEEEEEK!!!!"
shrieked Samantha,

hiding her face in her hands.

"**HELP!**" screamed Oliver, keeling over onto the floor in fright.

"**IT'S THE GHOST!!!**" yelled Jasper.

Oscar, who had been floating down the hall in front of us, pulled back into the shadows. His smile disappeared immediately.

"Wait!" said Dad, holding up his hands. "Everyone, listen. This ghost is friendly."

But no one listened. They all turned around and RAN.

"Oh dear," said Dad.

"I told you," I said.

Oscar gave a sad little sniff and began to glide away, back toward the dungeon below.

"Hey!" I called. "Oscar, come back!"

But Oscar didn't turn around. He floated all the way back down the hall and toward the dungeon.

"What a shame!" said Dad as we stood together in the now-empty hallway. "Poor Oscar."

"I told you!" I said again.

"You did," sighed Dad. "You were right, Isadora. We need to find a different way to introduce the ghost to the class."

We made our way back along the hall to the dungeon.

"Oscar!" I called as we hurried down the stone steps. "Where are you?"

"Are you in here again?" asked Dad, opening the cupboard door. We both peered into the darkness. There was the little silvery shape, trembling in the corner where it had been before.

"Oscar!" I said. "Come out! Don't be afraid!"

"But I am afraid," sobbed Oscar. "I'm afraid I'm never going to have any friends."

"You will!" I insisted. "We just have to find the right way to introduce you."

"And you already have two friends!" added Dad. "Me and Isadora."

Oscar sniffed. "That's true," he said,

cheering up a little. He uncurled himself and floated out of the cupboard.

"Right," said Dad. "We need to think of something quickly. Before the end of the field trip!"

"Yes!" I agreed. "We need to think of some way that Oscar can join in without anyone noticing that he is a ghost."

"Hmm . . . ," said Dad.

Pink Rabbit started to twitch his ears and tug at my prisoner costume. I looked down at my stripy legs and at the ball and chain attached to my ankle.

"I wonder . . . ," I began. "I wonder if there are any costumes in the castle that

Oscar would be able to wear. If we could find one with a hood, then it would hide his face, and no one would be able to tell he was a ghost."

"What a good idea!" said Dad.

Oscar started to jiggle up and down in the air excitedly. "I know where all the costumes are in the castle!" he said. "I have been living here for two hundred years, after all! I know there's a monk costume with a hood in the chapel, but—even better— there's another knight costume in the room where all the swords and shields are. It's got a metal helmet!"

"Perfect!" said Dad. "We need to get to

that room fast, in case the others decide to go there before us. Come on!"

Oscar, Pink Rabbit, and I followed Dad as he flew out of the dungeon and back up the steps.

"I'll show you the way!" said Oscar, whizzing ahead. We zoomed along the hallway, back through the throne room, and up a grand staircase to the first floor. We hurtled along a twisty corridor, past lots of paintings, and into a big room that had

hundreds of shiny swords and shields hanging on the walls.

Then I spotted the dress-up box in the corner of the room and ran to open it.

"Here it is!" I gasped, holding up a knight costume that was different from the ones Bruno had found earlier. This one had a helmet with a big plume of feathers sticking out of it.

"Wow!" said Dad. "That is fancy!"

Oscar floated into the costume, and I put the helmet onto his head.

"You need to remember to stay on the ground," I told him. "No rising up into the air!"

"Yes," agreed Dad. "That would give the secret away!"

Oscar sank to the ground.

"We need to find the others now," I said. "I wonder where they are."

Chapter Nine

After searching the castle for fifteen minutes, we found Miss Cherry and the rest of the class in the entrance hall.

"I'm telling you, it was a real ghost!" Miss Cherry was saying to the man in the ticket booth. "It chased us down the hallway!"

"It was coming to attack us!" said Jasper.

"Right," said the man in an amused sort of way.

Then Miss Cherry turned around and saw Dad and me. Her face took on a frightened look again.

"It's okay," said Dad. "There's no ghost. Look. It's gone."

Miss Cherry put her hand on her heart.

"Thank goodness for that!" she said. "But who's that child in the knight costume?"

"Oh, that's Oscar," said Dad. "He was lost and trying to find the . . . um . . . lunchroom. So I said he could come with us."

Miss Cherry looked at her watch.

"Ah, yes, lunch," she said. "I think lunch might be a good idea right now. Follow me, everyone!"

We all followed Miss Cherry to the lunchroom and sat at long wooden tables.

"That was the scariest thing I've ever seen!" said Zoe as she sat down next to me and opened her lunch box.

"Same," agreed Oliver. "I can't believe we saw a real ghost!"

Oscar sat next to me and didn't say anything. I hoped no one would notice that he didn't have a lunch box of his own. I handed him a sandwich under the table.

"I can't eat that!" he whispered. "Ghosts don't eat food!"

"Oh!" I said. "Of course! Well, maybe you should pretend to eat it anyway."

Oscar took the sandwich and put it in front of him on the table.

"So where are you from, Oscar?" Zoe asked.

"Um . . . ," began Oscar.

"Yeah, and which room did you get that knight costume from?" asked Bruno. "It's much better than mine!"

"So much better," agreed Sashi. "It has a real helmet!"

"I still haven't found a costume!" Samantha said. "I want to be a princess!"

"I know where the princess costume is!" said Oscar. "It's in the royal bedroom."

"Really?!" said Samantha excitedly. "How do you know that? You must have been around the whole castle already!"

"I have," said Oscar truthfully.

"Cool! What other costumes are there?" Jasper asked.

Oscar started to list all the different dress-up outfits that were hidden around the castle.

"I want the archer's outfit!" yelled Jasper. "I can be like Robin Hood!"

"Patience, please, Jasper," called Miss Cherry from the next table. "We'll get to see the archery room after lunch."

"The archery room?" asked Samantha. "What is that?"

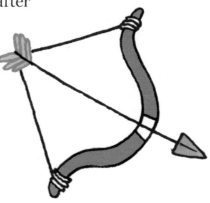

"It's the place where they keep all the bows and arrows," explained Oscar. "And there's a section where you are allowed to try them. It's really fun."

"Ooh," said Jasper. "I can't wait for that."

I stayed quiet and ate my lunch while my friends asked Oscar more questions about the castle. It was nice to see Oscar so happy. He was having such a good time telling everyone what he knew. They all seemed very impressed.

"You know a lot, Oscar," said Sashi as

we finished our lunches and stood up from the table. "You must be very smart!"

"Oh," said Oscar, looking pleased and embarrassed. "Well . . . I just have a lot of time on my hands!"

Chapter
Ten

After lunch we all followed Miss Cherry to the archery room, including Oscar. Jasper raced toward the dress-up box and pulled out the archer's outfit.

"I'm just like Robin Hood now!" he cried, putting it on over his clothes.

Then it was time for an archery lesson. A woman came in and showed us how to use

a bow and arrow. We had to shoot the arrow
across the room and try to hit the target
on the other side.

"It's really hard," said Dominic as
his arrow went flying up toward the
high ceiling.

"Really hard!" agreed Jasper. "Even with my archer's outfit on!"

Oscar was the last to have a turn.

"Wow!" said everyone after Oscar's arrow hit the bull's-eye. "Amazing!"

"Well done!" said the woman, sounding really impressed. "See if you can do it again!" She handed Oscar another arrow, and Oscar shot it right into the bull's-eye for the second time.

"Double wow!" said the woman. "You are really talented."

"Whoa!" said the class, and Jasper's eyes almost popped out of his head.

"You are awesome, Oscar!" he said.

Oscar looked down and shuffled his feet with embarrassment, but I could tell he was really pleased.

"I can teach you how to do it sometime, if you like," he offered.

Jasper nodded his head eagerly.

"Yes, please!" he said.

After archery we made our way upstairs and looked around some of the other rooms, including the one full of swords and shields, and the tall tower with one hundred steps leading up to it. Samantha found the princess outfit in the royal bedroom.

"It's time for the last room!" said Miss Cherry once we were back on the ground floor again. "It's the chapel. I think there's one more costume left in there too. Who isn't dressed up yet?"

"Me!" said Dominic. "I want to be a knight or an archer!"

"Oh dear, Dominic," said Miss Cherry. "I'm afraid it's more likely that you'll be a monk."

The chapel was a beautiful room with arched ceilings and lots of carvings covered in a thin layer of silver.

Connected to the chapel was another fancy room with a huge complicated-looking instrument in it.

"Oh!" said Dad. "An organ! I would love to be able to play the organ! Very gothic and vampire-y, don't you think?" He sat down on the seat and started to press the notes. A tuneless song came out, and everyone put their fingers in their ears.

"Dad," I hissed. "I don't think you're supposed to touch that!"

"It's all right," said a man who was standing nearby. "We encourage people to try the instruments. In fact," he said, gesturing toward the table next to him, "there are lots of medieval instruments for you to play here!" He picked up one and handed it to Oliver. "This is a lute," he said. "Try it out."

Oliver started to twang on the lute as the man handed out the rest of the

instruments to the class. There was a horn, a flute, a tambourine, a harp, a drum, a wooden recorder, and several others.

"I know how to play the recorder!" said Zoe.

"I want to play the tambourine!" said Sashi.

"Can I try the harp?" asked Samantha shyly.

Soon everyone in the class had an instrument to play. Oliver strummed his lute, Sashi banged her tambourine, Samantha plucked at her harp, Dominic blew on the flute, Zoe puffed on the recorder, Bruno honked on a trumpet, Jasper banged on a drum, I tootled on the horn, and Oscar played the organ.

"This is so much fun!" shouted Bruno. "It's like we're in a band!"

"It is!" yelled Sashi. "We should have band practice every week!"

"That would be so great!" cried Zoe. "We could put on a concert."

"I think you all might need a bit more practice before then," bellowed Dad, putting his fingers in his ears.

But there was one "person" who didn't seem to need any practice. Over the sound of all the squeaking, squawking, crashing instruments was the sound of the organ. And it was being played beautifully. A haunting, bewitching melody rang out over the noise as Oscar ran his silvery fingers up and down the keys. One by one my friends stopped playing their instruments and began to listen to the angelic sound of the organ.

"That is such a pretty song!" sighed Samantha as she put down her harp.

"Amazing," said Sashi.

"We definitely need Oscar for our band," said Bruno.

"Definitely," agreed Jasper.

Miss Cherry, who had closed her eyes to listen to the music, suddenly frowned and looked up.

"Who's Oscar?" she said.

Oscar's fingers stopped moving over the keys of the organ and came to rest slowly in his lap. He didn't say anything.

"Hang on," said Miss Cherry, counting all the children in the room. "This boy is not part of the class!" She narrowed her eyes at Dad. "Didn't you say you were taking him to the lunchroom?"

"Um . . . ," said Dad.

Miss Cherry started to look panicked.

"We must find his parents!" she wailed. "Or we might be accused of kidnapping!"

100

"We won't be accused of kidnapping,"
said Dad. "Oscar doesn't have any parents."

Miss Cherry looked confused, and
Oscar hung his head sadly.

"It's true," he said. "I don't have anyone."

"What do you mean?" asked Miss Cherry in bewilderment. "Everyone has someone."

"Not Oscar," I said, going over to where he was sitting at the organ and putting my hand on his shoulder. Miss Cherry, Dad, and the class all stared at us.

"There's something special about Oscar," I said. "He's . . . he's . . ."

"He's what?" asked Sashi.

"Tell us!" said Bruno.

"Ooh, is it a secret?" asked Zoe.

"Well, yes," I said. "Sort of. You have to promise not to scream or run away."

"Of course we won't run away!" scoffed Bruno. "Oscar is awesome!"

"Yes!" agreed Zoe. "We love Oscar! What could possibly be scary about him?"

"Exactly!" I said. "Nothing at all!"

Carefully I lifted the helmet from Oscar's head and put it on the floor. My friends and Miss Cherry gasped.

"Is that . . . is that . . . ?" they stuttered.

"It's the ghost we saw earlier," I explained. "But he's not scary. He's really nice. He just wants to make friends."

Bruno took a deep breath and stepped forward.

"I would love to be your friend, Oscar," he said. "I'm sorry I was scared of you before."

"I'm sorry too," said Zoe. "I should have gotten to know you before I decided to run away."

"Me too," agreed Sashi.

One by one my friends stepped forward to shake Oscar's silvery hand. Oscar beamed from ear to ear, and I could tell he was really happy.

"It's been lovely to meet you, Oscar," said Miss Cherry, taking her turn to shake his hand. "Definitely an experience I'm sure none of us will forget!" She looked down at her watch.

"Oh dear," she said. "We are running late for the bus. I am afraid it's time to go home. You all should take off your costumes."

"Oh no!" said Zoe.

"I don't want to go back yet," said Bruno.

"But what about Oscar?" asked Sashi. "We need him for our band!"

Oscar sat on the stool by the organ and hung his head. He seemed very sad again.

"I wish I could be in your band," he said. "Today has been the best day I've had in a very long time! I hope you will all visit again. It gets pretty lonely in this castle."

"I can only imagine," said Dad glumly.

I thought of our home, with Mom and Baby Honeyblossom and Pink Rabbit. I looked at Dad and knew we were thinking the same thing.

"I know," he said. "Why don't you come back with us? You can come and live in our vampire-fairy house. What do you think?"

"Oh yes!" I exclaimed. "We have a very nice attic with lots of nooks and crannies!"

"In fact, we are in need of a house ghost. All the best vampires have them," said Dad.

"Really?!" said Oscar. "You would really let me come and haunt your house?"

"Of course!" said Dad. "We are a ghost-friendly family."

Oscar smiled the biggest smile I had ever seen in my life, and the whole class cheered.

"That would be amazing," he said. "I would love that. It would be the best thing to happen to me in two hundred years!"

Family Tree

My mom,
Countess Cordelia
Moon

Baby Honeyblossom

My dad,
Count Bartholomew
Moon

Me!
Isadora Moon

Pink Rabbit

Sink your fangs into another
Isadora Moon adventure!

ISADORA MOON

Saves the Carnival

"What fun!" cousin Mirabelle whooped.

"You know what would make it even more fun?" said Dad as he smoothed his perfectly perfect slicked-back hair. "These bumper cars would be much improved if they had bat wings and could fly in the air."

"Oh no!" I said. "You promised: no more magic. Let's leave them as they are!"

"But bat wings would be amazing!" said Dad. "Vampire-bat cars! Oh, come on, just one more little spell!"

"Let's do it!" shouted Mirabelle as she screeched past us. I saw her let go of the wheel and take out her potion kit. Then she mixed something up at lightning speed and threw it into the air. The bumper cars transformed into sleek black bat-winged cars and began to rise upward.

Every Isadora Moon adventure is totally unique!

Harriet Muncaster

Harriet Muncaster, that's me! I'm the author and illustrator of Isadora Moon.

Yes, really! I love anything teeny-tiny, anything starry, and everything glittery.

New friends. New adventures.
Find a new series . . . just for you!

ISADORA MOON

For ballerina and fairy and vampire lovers

COMMANDER IN CHEESE

For adventurers

JULIAN'S WORLD
THE STORIES JULIAN TELLS

For storytellers

PUPPY PIRATES

For dog lovers

PuRRmaids

For mermaid and cat lovers

BALLPARK Mysteries

For sports fans

RHCB RHCBooks.com